CHEWY
LOUIE

by Howie Schneider

To Sophia Edith Schneider and,
of course, to Louie.

ISBN 0-439-36615-1

12 11 10 9 8 7 6 5 4   2 3 4 5 6/0

Printed in the U.S.A.   14

First Scholastic printing, October 2001

The illustrations were rendered in colored pencil.
The text type was set in Impress.
The display type was set in Helvetica Rounded.
Designed by Michael Russell

One day my father brought home
a little black puppy.

He was very cute and always hungry.
We called him Chewy Louie.

He ate everything we put in his bowl.

Then he ate the bowl.

My mother was very worried.

"He'll get sick," she said.

"He won't get sick," my father said.
"He's just a puppy."

Then he bought Louie a new bowl.

That one didn't make him sick either.

Louie slept with me in my bed at night.

When he wasn't eating my toys.

Louie ate my trains before they reached the station.

Then he ate the station.

My mother was very worried. My father
said he would buy me a new set of trains.

"He's just a puppy," he said.

One day Louie started to eat the back porch. My mother was horrified. My father was a little concerned, too.

"That's some puppy," he said.

We decided to take Louie to a vet.

The vet said to feed him more.
"He's just a growing puppy," he said.

Then he gave us the bill.

That night my father and mother
sat down to figure out what to do.
I was afraid they were going to
give Louie away.

My father hired a construction crew to
repair the house. My birthday party was
coming up soon and my mother wanted
the place to look nice.

"What a cute puppy," said one of the workmen.

They went inside to talk to my father about the job.

Then they came back out and saw
their truck.

Then they quit the job.

My father was furious. I thought he was
really going to send Louie away this time.

He decided to hire a trainer.

The trainer arrived the next day and immediately went to work.

And so did Louie.

Then my father had to hire another trainer.

She brought a guitar along and sang songs
to Louie about the error of his ways.

I think Louie liked her songs very much.

But he really loved her guitar.

We didn't have any more time to worry about Louie now. My birthday party was tomorrow and we all had to work hard to fix the place up. My mother wanted the party to be a big success.

But instead all her worst fears came true.
Louie was horrible.

I woke up the next morning feeling miserable. I knew now that we couldn't keep Louie. I decided to play one last game of fetch with him. Although it wasn't really fetch. I just threw the sticks and Louie ate them.

But not today! Louie brought the stick back
today. "Hey, Dad!" I shouted. "Look at Louie!
HE'S NOT CHEWING ANYMORE!"

Even my mother was impressed.

Louie was changing. He was getting older and bigger every day.

He didn't even eat my toys anymore.

My mother still worried.
"Do you think he's stopped chewing for good?" she asked.

"Of course," said my father.

"He's not a puppy anymore."